Why Sydney Can't Sit In the Front Seat

by Samuel Martin, Jr
Illustrated by Iwan D

Dedication

This book is dedicated to Talia, Sydney, Nakia, Briana, and all the beautiful little boys and girls and their Funbears who ask to sit in the front seat.

Enjoy this book from the very first picture
Until all the words are done

But the words in *BIG COLORS* say with *EXTRA FEELING*

To make your reading *REALLY* fun

"C'mon Sydney, "said Mommy from the top of the stairs.

"It's time to go." Sydney was **excited**. They were going to lunch and she couldn't wait. She ran to the kitchen to get her teddy bear, Funbear Grey. She **never** went anywhere without him.

"No running in the house Sydney," Mother said as she came down the stairs. "You know better. I wouldn't want you to get hurt."

"Yes Mommy" said Sydney, slowing down. Running was fun but it was *always* best to obey Mommy.

They quickly got their things together and walked toward the car. Sydney's eyes got so big. " Mommy, Mommy, may I sit in the front seat today? *Please, please?*"

Mommy looked at Sydney and smiled. She quietly opened the back seat door of the car and motioned Sydney to get in. Sydney frowned and began to whine, "Why can't I **ever** sit in the front seat? I'm big enough."

"I'm sorry Sydney," said Mommy, "but you won't be big enough to sit in the front with me for a few years." Sydney grabbed Funbear Grey and climbed in the back.

She carefully buckled Funbear Grey in his seatbelt. Then she sat in her child's seat and fastened her own seatbelt. She folded her arms and frowned.

"I never get to sit in the front seat. Never!" Then she closed her eyes and went to sleep.

She slept and slept and slept. Then she awoke to someone calling her name.

"Sydney. Sydney, wake up precious."

Sydney opened her eyes and started to laugh and giggle. To her surprise there were two giant balloons smiling at her. "*Who* are you?" she giggled.

"We're airbags," both of the balloons said together.

"*Airbags*?" Sydney said looking quite confused. She had never spoken to an airbag before.

"Yes. I'm Larry the left airbag, and he is Ronald the right airbag. We are the main reason why you can't sit in the front seat."

Sydney crossed her arms and began to frown. She made sure Funbear Grey crossed his arms too. They were both quite upset.

"**You're the reason** I can not sit in the front seat? Why are you being **mean to me**?"

16

"*Oh Sydney*," said Larry the left airbag, "We're not being mean to you. In fact, we're your friends. We are here to protect you."

"Protect me?" Sydney said with her bottom lip still poked out.

"How?" she asked. Her teddy bear, Funbear Grey's lip was poked out too.

"Oh Sydney," said Larry the left airbag, "**We** protect in different ways. **If** you were to get in an accident, I would come out of Mommy's steering wheel and act as a cushion to protect her from harm. "

"Yes, yes," said Ronald the right airbag. And if your big sister was sitting up front with Mommy, I would come out of the dash board like a *big pillow* and protect her from bumping her head on the windshield. But I can *only* protect you if you are a certain age or weight, otherwise it's a good chance that the force from me coming out of the dashboard can do more harm than good."

Sydney put her hands over her mouth in amazement, and her teddy bear, Funbear Grey, did too. "**Wow**! Is **that** where you live? You live in the dashboard and steering wheel?"

"Why yes", said Larry the left airbag. "The dashboard **and** steering wheel is where we live."

"Yes, yes, yes", said Ronald the right air bag. "We just wait and wait and wait until we are needed. But we hope you **never, never, never** need us, because you are precious."

"What does precious mean?" said Sydney rubbing her eyes.
She was starting to get sleepy. The teddy bear was getting
sleepy too.

"Precious means that you are *special* and that you are *loved*," said Larry the left airbag. "Yes, yes, yes," said Ronald the right airbag. "We protect and love you, just like your Mommy protects and loves you.

Now, we are going to say goodbye so you can go to sleep, and when you wake up, you can tell your Mommy that you love her too."

Sydney and the teddy bear waved goodbye to Larry and Ronald the airbags. Then they both yawned an **extra** good yawn and fell into an **extra** good sleep.

When Sydney awoke, the airbags were gone and her Mommy was driving the car. Sydney sat up in her car seat. Her eyes *wide open* with excitement.

"Mommy, Mommy, while I was asleep I met the airbags."

"You *did*?" Mommy said smiling.

"Yes. They live in the dashboard and steering wheel, and they explained to me why I can't sit in the front seat with you."

Mommy smiled again and looked at Sydney. "And tell Mommy why you can't sit in the front seat."

Sydney raised both arms in the air and said, "It's because you love me."

"That's right," said Mommy laughing.

Then Sydney blew her Mommy a big kiss. "*And I love you too*."

And on the inside, Funbear Grey just *laughed and laughed and laughed*.

The End.

But wait...

Here's a fun rhyme to remember the backseat rules.

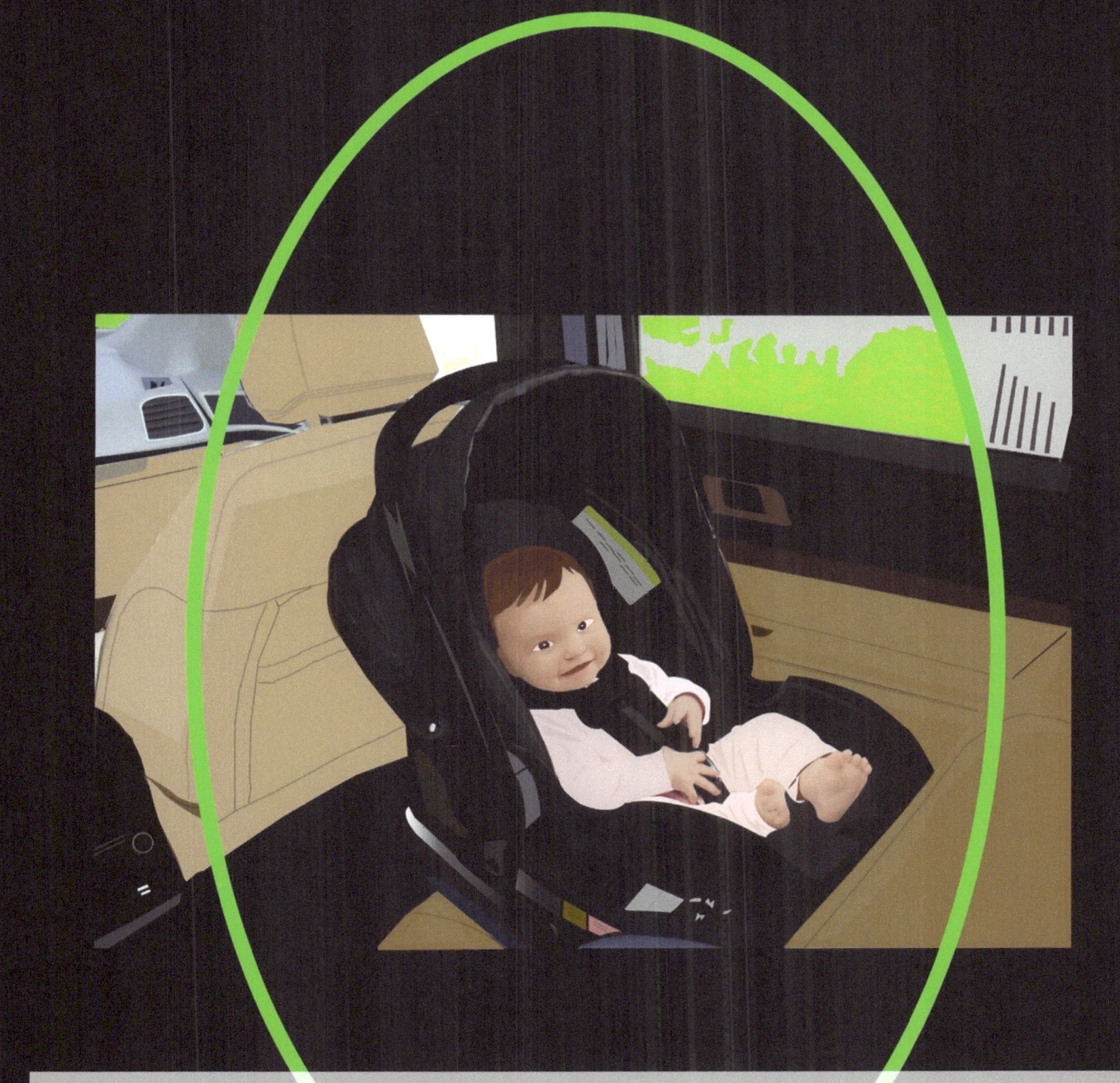

Babies sit in rear facing seats
From birth until the age of 2 is allowed
Or until baby has grown a bit too heavy
Which will be around 35 pounds

Toddlers must sit in the forward facing seats
No longer are they turned around
With a harness that comes over both of their shoulders
They must weigh 40 through 65 pounds

Once kids get a little bit taller
And really start to grow
Between 8 and 12 or until they are 4 feet 9"
A booster seat is the way to go

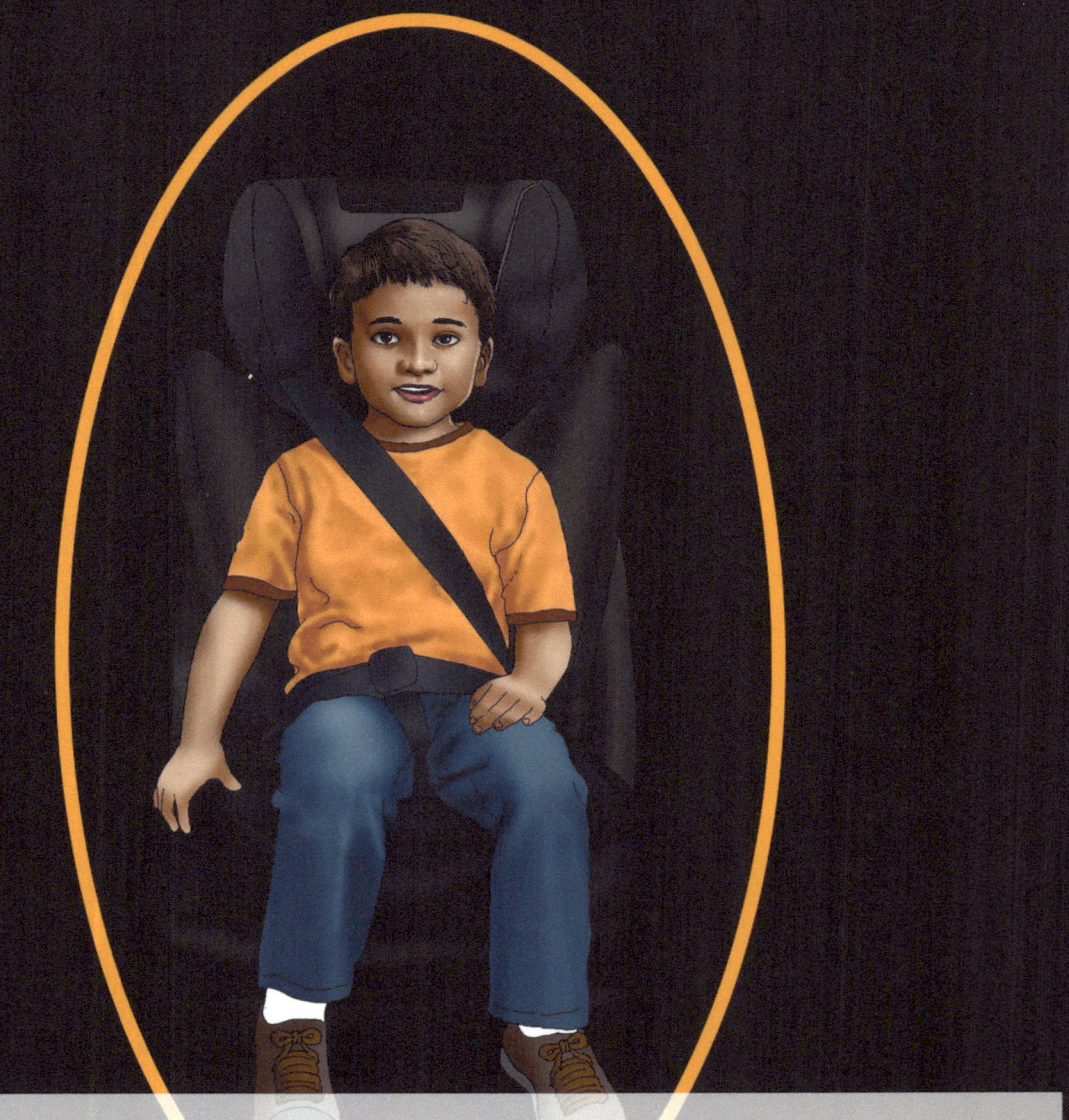

Once the lap and shoulder belts fit properly
And everything's ok
Kids no longer need any safety seats
But until 13, in the back we must stay.
Hooray!!!!

Be sure to listen to my favorite songs,

1. Shake and Wiggle
2. This is a castle
3. The Clapping Game, and others on Taliakids.com and
   YouTube.

See you next time.
Bye, Bye!